Hudson Bay
QUEBEC
James Bay
A
D
ONTARIO
Lake Superior
Lake Huron
TORONTO
L. Ontario
L. Michigan
L. Erie

Published in Canada
and the USA in 2014
by Groundwood Books



Groundwood Books / House of Anansi Press
110 Spadina Avenue, Suite 801, Toronto, Ontario M5V 2K4
or c/o Publishers Group West
1700 Fourth Street, Berkeley, CA 94710

We acknowledge for their financial support of our publishing program
the Canada Council for the Arts, the Government of Canada through
the Canada Book
Fund (CBF) and the Ontario
Arts Council.

For my mom,
Gloria Buchanan, and
in memory of my dad,
Bud Buchanan — LC

For my dad,
Malcolm James
— MJ

Canada Council for the Arts
Conseil des Arts du Canada

ONTARIO ARTS COUNCIL
CONSEIL DES ARTS DE L'ONTARIO

Library and Archives Canada Cataloguing in Publication
Croza, Laurel, author
From there to here / by Laurel Croza ; illustrated by Matt
James.
Issued in print and electronic formats.
ISBN 978-1-55498-365-0 (bound). –
ISBN 978-1-55498-366-7 (html)
I. James, Matt, illustrator II. Title.
PS8605.R698F76 2014 jC813'.6 C2013-905645-9
C2013-907136-9

The illustrations were done in
India ink on panel.
Design by Michael Solomon
Printed and bound in China

# FROM THERE TO HERE

Laurel Croza

PICTURES BY

Matt James

GROUNDWOOD BOOKS
HOUSE OF ANANSI PRESS
TORONTO BERKELEY

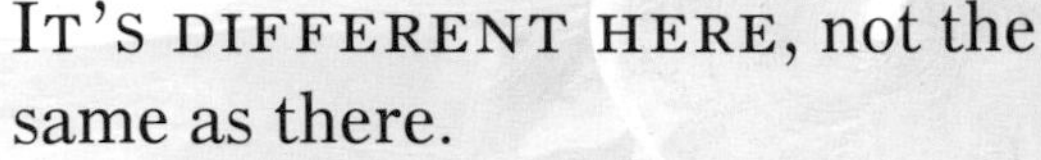

IT'S DIFFERENT HERE, not the same as there.

There. Dad drove home each day to eat lunch with us.

Here. Dad isn't home until supper. Mom calls it dinner now.

There. Dad helped build a dam, stretching across the Saskatchewan River.

Here. Dad helps build a highway, stretching across Toronto. Lanes going west and lanes going east.

East. That's the direction we came — from there to here — all the way by train. Pulling out of Saskatoon, rattling faster and faster on the tracks, swaying everyone to sleep. Except me, my forehead pressed against the window, listening to the train whistle, "Gooooood-bye."

There. We lived on a road. A graveled and oiled road, carved into the middle of the bush. A road without a name.

Here. We live on a street. An asphalted and sidewalked street, paved into the middle of the city. A street with a name. Birch Street. I don't see any birch trees. They must be hiding in the backyards behind the fences.

There. Plenty of birch trees — and pine and spruce and poplar — a forest of trees for a backyard. No fences. Or front yards. The trailers sat roosted right alongside the road, curtains open. Nobody locked their doors.

Here. Green grass lawns and flower gardens and driveways first, and then the houses, drapes closed. We keep forgetting to lock our door.

There. A tarp of twinkle, twinkle little stars hung high above our trailers. And on some nights, a special show when aurora borealis shimmered in the sky, swirling and twirling, dancing just for us.

Here. No stars, no northern lights. The street lamps in a straight row — standing at attention — glaring down the dark.

There. A brush fire upriver, the smell of home.

Here. The carpet,
it smells new.

There.
We traveled
in a pack — all
the kids, so long as
we could keep up —
down our road, through
the forest, past the creek,
towards the hill, howling
like wolves, "Last one to the
top is a dirty rotten egg."

Here. Doug has made his own friends.

And today they took a bus to the Canadian National Exhibition.

"Why can't I go?" I asked.

"Because you're not old enough," he said.

Well. I'm old enough to
watch my little brothers and
my little sister while Mom
unpacks more boxes.

My eyes are on Michael, asleep on the couch, and Stephen, stuck to the TV — "Th-th-th-that's all, folks!" — and Kathie, cutting and pasting frogs from *National Geographic*.

But my ears are waiting for a knock on the door.

Knock-knock.

Who's here?

Anne. That's who.

Anne, who lives kitty-corner to me. Anne, who was waiting beside the moving truck the afternoon we arrived.

"How old are you?" she asked.

"Eight, almost nine," I answered.

"How old are you?" I asked.

"Eight, almost nine," she answered.

There. Only me, my age, on my road.

"Ready?" Anne says.

"Ready," I say.

Here. Anne and me on our bikes — down our street, through the church parking lot, past the apartment buildings towards Yonge Street and lunch at the Red Barn — pedaling faster and faster. The Toronto air rushes to greet me, tugging up the corners of my mouth. Anne is smiling, too.

It was different there.
Not the same as here.

NUNA
NORTHWEST TERRITORIES
C
A
N
SASKATCHEWAN
ALBERTA
MANITOBA
Winnipeg
UNITED STAT